As usual, Martin was first to finish all the
math problems.
Now he had nothing to do.
He looked out the window.
He played with his pencils.
He wiggled a loose tooth with his tongue.
It was Martin's first loose tooth.

The tooth fell out.

"Look at my tooth!" Martin said.

"It's ugly," said Cynthia.

"No, it's not," said John.

"That's what a tooth is supposed to look like."

Martin and the Tooth Fairy

by Bernice Chardiet and Grace Maccarone
pictures by G. Brian Karas

SCHOLASTIC INC.

New York   Toronto   London   Auckland   Sydney

To Steve
G.M.

To Murray Raybin, D.D.S.
B.C.

For Marissa and Michelle
G.B.K.

Text copyright © 1990 by Grace Maccarone
and
Bernice Chardiet.
Illustrations copyright © 1990 by Chardiet Unlimited Inc.
All rights reserved. Published by Scholastic Inc.
Produced by Chardiet Unlimited, Inc.

ISBN 0-590-43305-9

12 11 10 9 8 7 6 5   2 3 4 5/9

Printed in U.S.A.   08

First Scholastic printing, January 1991

Martin walked to the waste basket.
"Wait!" said Bunny. "Don't throw it out.
You're supposed to put it under your
pillow for the Tooth Fairy.
She'll take your tooth and give you
money while you're sleeping."

After school, Martin showed the tooth to his parents.

"Our boy is growing up," said his mother.

"Before you know it, he'll be shaving," said his father.

"No, I won't," said Martin.

"I'm growing a beard like Uncle Steve."

That night, Martin put the tooth under
his pillow just as Bunny had told him.
When he woke the next morning,
4 shiny quarters were in its place.

"I got 4 quarters!" Martin said at school.
"Wow!" said John. "The Tooth Fairy gives
me only 1 quarter."
"I have an idea," said Martin. "I'll give
you 2 quarters for your next tooth.
The Tooth Fairy will give me 4 quarters
when I put it under my pillow. We'll
both make money!"
"It's a deal," said John.

"I don't want the Tooth Fairy flying
around my house," said Cynthia.
"You can have my tooth, too."

Martin wanted to make more money.
At lunchtime, he made a sign and put it
on his lunch tray.
The sign said:

    MARTIN'S TOOTH MARKET
    2 QUARTERS FOR 1 TOOTH

That day, Martin made deals with Brenda
and Michael and Daniel and Tanya.

Sammy Cooper would not make a deal.
"The Tooth Fairy doesn't get my teeth,"
he said. "I'm saving them to make a
model of a mouth."
"Yech," said Cynthia.

"You can have my next tooth," said
Raymond. "But I want my money now."
Martin thought about it.
He had some money in his piggy bank.

"Okay," said Martin. "I'll pay you
tomorrow."
"I want my money, too," said Cynthia.
"Me, too," said John.
"Okay," said Martin.
But Martin was worried.
If this idea didn't work, he'd have no
money left in his piggy bank.

A week passed by.
But nobody had lost a tooth yet.
Then Martin saw Cynthia.
"What are you looking at?" Cynthia
shouted.
"I think you have a loose tooth,"
Martin said.
Cynthia covered her mouth.
She mumbled through her fingers,
"Go away!"

Martin tried to take Cynthia's hand away.
All of a sudden, out popped her tooth.
They both grabbed for it.
Cynthia's hand was there first.

"I changed my mind," she said.
"You can't have my tooth."
"A deal's a deal," said Martin.

"I'll tell my mother," said Cynthia.
"She'll make you give it back.
Here are your stupid quarters!"
So Martin took his 2 quarters.
Now he waited for someone else's
tooth to fall out.

The next day, at lunch, Raymond's tooth fell into his spaghetti.

"Great!" said Martin. "I'll take it!"

"I don't know," said Raymond.

"I think that this tooth is worth more than 2 quarters.

It's a molar. See how big it is?"

"A deal's a deal," said Martin.

"Three quarters or the deal is off," Raymond said.

Martin would not give in.
But Raymond would not give in either.
He left the tooth on top of his desk all
day for Martin to see.
Martin saw it during reading.
Martin saw it during math.

Martin even saw it while he fed the
class's goldfish.

"I can't stand it anymore," said Martin.

"I'll give you 3 quarters.

But don't tell anyone else, or everyone
will ask for more money."

That night, Martin put Raymond's tooth
under his pillow.
Maybe the Tooth Fairy gives more money
for molars, Martin thought.
He was so excited. It took him a long
time to fall asleep.

The next morning, Martin slept late.
"You'd better hurry. You'll be late for
school," his mother called.
Then Martin remembered Raymond's tooth.
He reached under his pillow.
Raymond's tooth was still there!

Martin walked into the kitchen.
"You don't look good," his mother said.
"Are you feeling all right?"
"Why didn't the Tooth Fairy come last
night?" Martin asked.

"Did you lose another tooth?" asked his mother.

"No," said Martin, "Raymond did."

"What are you doing with Raymond's tooth?" Martin's mother asked.

"I put his tooth under my pillow, but the Tooth Fairy didn't take it.
Maybe it was too big and ugly,"
Martin said.
"I don't think that was why,"
his mother said.
Martin thought some more.
"I guess she only comes when it's your own."
"I guess so," said Martin's mother.
Martin was sad. Then he had an idea.
Maybe he could get Raymond to buy his tooth back.

While Martin was looking for Raymond in the schoolyard, John came over and said, "I heard you gave Raymond 3 quarters for his tooth. I want 3 quarters, too, or the deal is off!"

"Okay," Martin said. "The deal is off.
Give me my 2 quarters back, and you can
keep your tooth."
"Okay," said John.

Bunny came over next.
"I want 3 quarters for my tooth, too,"
she said.
"No," said Martin. "But if you want to
call off the deal, that's all right with me."
"Okay," said Bunny.

Now she could keep her own tooth
and put it under her own pillow.
The Tooth Fairy would come to her
own room. Bunny was glad. She didn't
care about the money.

One by one, the boys and girls asked
for 3 quarters. It was Martin's lucky day.
Martin let them keep their teeth.
And Martin got to keep his money.
Even Raymond wanted his tooth back.
That day at lunch, Martin put a new sign
on his tray. It said:

OUT OF BUSINESS!